The Unfaithful Spouse

Destiny O. Emmanuel

authorHOUSE®

AuthorHouse™
1663 Liberty Drive
Bloomington, IN 47403
www.authorhouse.com
Phone: 1 (800) 839-8640

Published by AuthorHouse   07/22/2016

ISBN: 978-1-5049-5524-9 (sc)
ISBN: 978-1-5049-5523-2 (hc)
ISBN: 978-1-5049-5525-6 (e)

Library of Congress Control Number: 2015916691

Print information available on the last page.

Any people depicted in stock imagery provided by Thinkstock are models, and such images are being used for illustrative purposes only. Certain stock imagery © Thinkstock.

This book is printed on acid-free paper.

Because of the dynamic nature of the Internet, any web addresses or links contained in this book may have changed since publication and may no longer be valid. The views expressed in this work are solely those of the author and do not necessarily reflect the views of the publisher, and the publisher hereby disclaims any responsibility for them.

Contents

1

The Unruly King

It was a blissful day as usual in Imoku community. The community was quite a large one, but many of the houses were mud houses with raffia roofs. Only a few houses were covered with zinc, of which the king's palace was one. Goats and chickens strayed freely. Several children also ran freely with only their pants on, and some were nude, with their fingers in their mouths. The rural dwellers were notable farmers, fishermen, and craftsmen.

King Zamadora, the ruler of Imoku community, was influential, feared, and respected by all in the community and its environs. To the community dwellers, the fear of His Majesty was the beginning of good judgment because of his tyrannical rule. He was also seen as the final arbiter. He had just ordered the execution of Ladi, the drummer, for having dared to chat with his only daughter under a mango tree.

After the execution, the inhabitants mourned for countless days. The community was quiet. Everyone felt his absence, especially the children. Ladi was a good storyteller. He often gathered little children underneath the big mahogany tree at the back of his house for moonlight tales. Occasionally, some of them

dozed off while listening. His children, three boys and two girls, also enjoyed their father's stories.

His Majesty had summoned Ladi that ill-fated evening and had ordered his messenger and two of his palace guards to bring him to his palace. Immediately he was notifies, he knew he would not see the dawn of the following day, the reason being that he had faced the king's court the previous day and was found guilty. He entered and picked his cap with the thought that it would be sent back to his wife after his execution. His wife wept bitterly as he was set to go with the king's messengers. She beseeched him not to go, but to no avail.

"Who will take care of us, my husband? Please do not go with them," Yoma begged.

"My dear, the gods of our forefathers will protect you and my children," Ladi replied as he tried to encourage his wife. Yoma held him by the leg while the children clung to him. They held on to him in tears and loud cries as the warriors dragged him away to the forbidden forest, where he was to be executed. The community dwellers watched helplessly as he was being dragged away.

After a long wait that seemed like eternity, his cap was sent to his wife. She wailed and wept uncontrollably. The women sympathized with her. Mama Bonboy lent a hand by preparing a sumptuous meal, which she declined. But her little child, who seemed not to understand the tragedy that had befallen her father, ate hungrily. It was a cold and grief-stricken

night in the neighborhood. Even the birds refused to chirp and the cocks crowed in a sorrowful rhythm. The moon was ashamed of the king's act and refused to smile on the community. Yoma cried till dawn.

Soku, the famous but poor fisherman, was sad when he learned about the unfortunate incident.

"Oh Death! Why have you come to take away a good man from us?" he lamented as he entered the deceased's small compound.

He sympathized and tried to console Yoma. After a while, he brought out the two big fishes he had caught and gave them to her. Mama Bonboy accepted the fishes on behalf of her bereaved friend. Ladi's wife could only nod to acknowledge his kind gestures.

Soku, on getting home, wept bitterly and cursed the king silently. Soku and Ladi had been very close before his death. His wife, Mira, consoled and begged him to eat, but he refused. He retired to bed and was deep in thought until the wee hours of the morning when he finally fell asleep.

Soku was a very simple man with a good heart. His wife was tall and dark-complexioned with perfect straight legs. She had a pointed nose and looked like a Fulani. Her eyes were light brown and mysterious like the quiet waters of a deep, glittery, morning stream. But she was an arrogant woman and always ready to foment trouble with anyone at the slightest provocation. In spite of her horrid character, her husband's affection for her grew daily.

Soku woke up at a time when the morning sun was smiling up in the sky. He looked worn out and worried.

"Is this the time your mates do wake up?" his wife asked in a scornful voice.

He made a great effort to sit up on the bamboo bed, yawning emphatically while his wife watched him with disdain.

"Woman, have you no respect for the dead?" he asked courteously.

"What has that got to do with us?" she asked angrily. "Let the dead be and the living with themselves."

"Woman, can't I have peace in my own house anymore?" he flung back at her. He stood up, picked up his chewing stick from the edge of the small window that made available little ventilation, and stuck it in his mouth. He was still for a moment as if trying to decide on what to do next and then walked out to the backyard.

"I am talking to you and you are walking away?" Mira snapped.

Some minutes later he strolled in and demanded his breakfast.

"I am very hungry. You know I did not eat last night. Please, can I have some food?"

"Why not eat me? Eh! Eat me," she hissed, "so the whole world would know that you are hungry."

"But I brought some fishes home yester-night," he said defensively, looking into his frustrated wife's eyes.

"*Fish!* Did I hear you say *fish?* You are not even ashamed to say you brought some fishes home," retorted his wife.

"I know it is not my fault for the fact that I did my best," her husband fired back.

"So, you did your best? Hmm, I can see." At that, she sprang on her feet and seized her husband by the wrapper he was tying. "Look at me, I am getting emaciated, and God knows I was fatter when you married me."

"Fatter indeed. In fact, you were fatter than a broom stick," he said frowning as he tried to loosen her grip.

"Look at you, say whatever you like. Sooner or later, I will find another man. You fool!" she cursed.

He was angry and smacked her violently on her left cheek. She screamed wildly and fell violently on the clay pots on the floor. She stood up and grabbed her husband's wrapper again, as she hurled insults at him. He ignored her and made an effort to walk away, but she would not let him. Before he could do away with her hand from his wrapper, she had spat in his face. This infuriated him, and he slapped her again and again until she let go of him. She leaped at him. They both exchanged blows, and he forced her hold off and pushed her on the bamboo bed.

"I do not blame you. If not for my father *that forcefully gave me to you*, I would not have been married to you. You are a shameless man!" she thundered as her husband hurriedly left the room.

2

The Secret Romance

Mira cried as she made her way to the palace to allege Soku. She met the king in a meeting with his chiefs. Without listening to her, King Zamadora ordered his guards to bring Soku to the palace, dead or alive.

The guards obeyed and immediately left for Soku's house, where they found him relaxing on his cane chair. He was surprised to see them moving like warriors set in battle and advancing toward his compound. Before he could sit up, they had pounced on him and beaten him black and blue. His eyes were swollen and bloodshot. His body ached as he wailed in agony for mercy. He shivered with the fear of the unknown as he was being dragged in the mud along the footpath to the palace. Passersby pitied him because they feared for his return.

On arriving at the palace, he greeted the king and lay on the ground faced down. He was surprised when he caught a glimpse of his wife kneeling down before the king. He wondered what his wife might have done wrong to the king. He was too frightened to lift his head up. When the king finally spoke, he could not believe his ears when he learned that it was his wife who had reported him to the king. One of

the chiefs asked Mira to continue from where she had stopped.

"And he punched me on the face and on my breast and kicked me in my stomach and—" she sobbed as she reeled out her own part of the story.

"But you told him what a married woman should never utter to the man who struggled to pay her bride price. You said that you would look for another man. It's never said," one of the chiefs who were present rebuked her.

"Not even when he is, in spite of everything, your husband," another chief cut in.

"Oh, come off it. You are all old fools with gray hair," King Zamadora shouted at the chiefs. "Is that how to pass judgment?"

The chiefs chuckled, looking down on the floor with dropped shoulders. They were not surprised at the king's action toward them.

"And you, what audacity have you to beat your wife? Under no circumstances should you lay your filthy hands on her again, or I shall have you stripped naked and flogged at the village square."

Soku looked up and immediately dropped his face again to avoid any eye contact with the king.

"You are an irresponsible idiot," he said, pointing his horsetail emphatically at Soku.

Mira smiled mischievously as she covered her face with her hands, pretending to sob.

"Now, you can go home. She will be right behind you," he concluded. "More so, she needs treatment."

The chiefs glanced at each other in a familiar way. Soku jumped up. He prostrated before the king again and again. There was a look on his face that turned Soku cold, and he moved silently backward until he was out of sight.

A few minutes later, King Zamadora discharged the chiefs and afterward ordered Mira to come with him to his private room. He sat down majestically on the bamboo bed covered with fine white linen. He was dazed by her looks. He patted the space beside him on the bed for her to sit. She was skeptical about what to do.

"You are beautiful. Has your husband ever told you that? Do you know you are pretty?" He cajoled with a beaming smile.

"Thank you, my lord," she responded with an uncomfortable smile.

"Have you been told before that you are a fallen angel from heaven? Come on, move closer, my dear, and I will make you one of my queens. Come and sit on the bed with me! My gracious cherub," he persuaded.

There was no response from her. She stared at her big toe as if she were seeing it for the first time.

"Are you shy?" he asked softly.

Quietly and slowly, she walked toward the king and sat beside him.

"I have been doing the talking since, not even a word from you. Why not say something?" he asked romantically, taking her hand and caressing it lightly.

"My lord, I am your subject. Do with me as you wish," she uttered softly.

"I yearn for you to be my companion. I had dreamt about you before the gods of the land brought you to the palace," he pleaded with a passionate voice.

She smiled and nestled closer to the king. The king lay with her and afterward, she wrapped her wrapper around her slim waist and walked out of the palace unnoticed.

Soku waited patiently for his wife to return that cold evening till midnight when he fell asleep. The sound of Mira opening the door woke him up.

"My sweetheart, I am so sorry for all that has happened," he apologized, but his wife would not listen to him. She hissed and walked straight to the bed.

Her husband did all he could to restore peace between them but to no avail. Soku invited some of Mira's family members and relatives to mediate between them but she would not compromise.

The amorous affair between the king and Soku's wife turned out to be an occasional schedule. She sneaked in and out of the palace to satisfy their sexual urges at any available opportunity. Each time Mira visited the palace, she often demanded for one thing or the other. It was either she requested for some amount of money, or she wanted a particular cloth she had seen on one or two of her friends. The king always granted her requests.

… … … … … … … … … … …

Ughele community was a confluence district to Imoku. It was time for the Ogoje festival, which was often celebrated yearly. The dwellers of Ughele community were getting prepared for the forth-coming festival with much enthusiasm. Each time it was being celebrated, people from all walks of life came from far and near to join in the festivity. It was always an interesting occasion. There was always enough to eat and drink. Palm wine was always in excess, and the careless drinkers would not hesitate to get intoxicated. The bachelors used the opportunity to find their future partners on this memorable day, so also the spinsters. A large number of Imoku indigenes moved to Ughele for the festival.

Soku could not resist the temptation of being there. His wife refused to go with him. He had pleaded with her the night before to accompany him, but she stubbornly turned him down. Her mind was miles away on her hidden agenda.

The celebration lasted all night, and everyone watched in admiration. The dancers and wrestlers entertained everyone in attendance. The masquerades plummeted in an extraordinary acrobatic fashion. Soku and others danced and cheered. He had merely drunk two cups of palm wine when he dozed off.

He awakened when nearly everyone had left the arena of the gala. At the sound of the first cock crow, he jumped up, cleansed his eyes with the edge of his dirty cloth, and shook his head.

He walked unsteadily to his cousin's home in Ughele. He was warmly received. He had his bath and chatted with him for some time. His cousin prepared him a sumptuous meal for breakfast. After the meal, he hastily left for home.

3

The False Allegation

Soku greeted some men on his way home as he walked past them.

"Good morning, my people," he hailed.

"Good morning," they responded cheerfully as he walked away.

"Is that not the man sharing his wife with the king?" asked Johnny, the community drunkard.

"Ha! It is not from my mouth you will hear that the king farted," one of the people walking by exclaimed.

"How do you mean?" others asked in whispers.

"My ears have not heard that the king farted," the oldest among the group whispered and walked away.

"Let him go. He is at all times frightened of the king," one of the young men said and urged Johnny to give them details of the clandestine affair.

Johnny felt very important. He majestically leaned on a nearby tree. By now everyone was quiet and keen on listening to him.

"You all know I have to see the end of the palm wine at Mama Akpan's place before I leave each day for home." He paused and staggered backward and

forward as if he was being controlled by the gentle early morning breeze.

"Yes? Yes?" One of the gossips encouraged him to go on with his gist.

"As I left Mama Akpan's kiosk to go and see my concubine—do not inform the king that I have a secret lover, or else—." He stopped momentarily and looked at his colleagues with one eye closed.

"Or else, he will make you another scapegoat and behead you," Adisa, whose wife was a bosom friend to Mira, joked.

They all burst into a rapturous laughter.

"You who cannot feed your beautiful wife let alone keep a concubine. You are going to die very soon," teased another.

"That one you called my wife is too lazy and arrogant for my liking. She does not know how to cook "oporoko" soup. And to make matters worse, she is so filthy. She is—," Johnny complained.

"I am scared of our king snatching my lover from me with his wealth and position," he finally said.

They all laughed again.

"As I was saying, before this housefly interrupted," he said sarcastically, pointing at the first man that interrupted him and waving his right hand as if he was waving a fly off.

"Continue with your story," they chorused as if nothing interested them about him.

"Because when I arrived at my sweetheart's place, she was not around. After waiting for a while,

I decided to take the footpath at the back of the palace leading to my house." He stopped again and looked from one person to another and finally rested his eyes on Adisa.

"What then happened?" they all asked, anxiously waiting to hear more.

"I saw Soku's wife sneaking out of the king's private room through the backyard," he said. "She was tiptoeing like a cat in the dark."

"Oh no! Poor Soku. Some women nowadays are not trustworthy," Adisa said pityingly.

"If you trust a woman and she is unfaithful, she will lead you to an untimely grave. After all, our king is wealthy while Soku is not," the drunkard added.

"Yes! Most women are unable to resist material things. If wealth grows on trees, some greedy women will get married to monkeys," Adisa reiterated.

They all laughed and had pity on him. As they were about to part for the day's work, Johnny looked at Adisa and smiled mischievously. Adisa asked what the sudden mischievous look was all about.

"Birds of the same feathers flock together," Johnny answered.

"Yes! Evil communication corrupts good manners," Maye said and walked away.

At once, Adisa's mind flew to his lovely wife at home. He thought of locking her up in her room, so that the randy king would not be able to see her, let alone have an affair with her. He carried this thought in his mind until he got home. His wife greeted him

as soon as he arrived, but he did not respond. He went straight to bed. He had a sleepless night thinking about his wife, and he woke up with anger in his heart.

The next day, his wife dressed up, ready for the market, and as she bade him goodbye, he stared at her for a minute, from her hair down to her toes and finally said, "Good-bye."

Barely had she taken five steps than he called her back.

"Come! Come! I say come back here," he fired, and his wife turned round and walked gracefully up to him.

"See, how you are walking, can't you walk like a married woman?" he shouted at her.

"How are married woman expected to walk?" she asked rudely.

"If you ask me that kind of question again, I will let loose the anger in my heart at you," he answered.

"But the way I walk has not changed since we got married!" she pleaded, wondering what could have gone wrong with her husband overnight.

Her husband mimicked her and asked with scorn, "Must you always shake your waist and body when you walk?"

"My husband, I hope you did not wake up on the wrong side of the bed this morning?" she asked suspiciously.

"By the way, are you going to pass by the palace road?" her husband questioned.

"Where else do I pass to the market if not the road beside the palace?" his wife answered angrily and turned to leave.

He cautioned her to stop and never walk out on him again. This she did momentarily.

"It is not proper for the knee to wear a cap when the head is available. I am your husband, and I deserve to be duly respected."

His wife was taken aback at her husband's behavior. Since they got married, her husband had never shouted at her.

He pointed his right finger at her face and said, "From this moment on, you must not take that route to the market again."

"But you know that is the fastest route to the market," she pleaded.

"Fastest or slowest, you must not take that route again," he warned again.

"How would you expect me to forgo a fast route?" his wife asked angrily.

"*Okay!* No wonder," he said scratching his Afro hair with the chewing stick he was chewing.

"No wonder what? How do you mean?" she probed.

"I have always heard that the antelope says it was never angry with the hunter who shot at it, but with the dog that drove it from its hiding place," he said.

"And what has that got to do with what we are saying?" she inquired, looking more serious.

"A lot, a lot, I say. You want to go and see the king just as your friend sneaks in and out of the palace every night," he said.

"My friend?" she asked slowly, looking puzzled.

"Yes! Your friend, Mira, of course," he said and made to leave through the back door.

Adisa's wife was dumbfounded. She carefully took a seat on the bamboo chair and beckoned her husband to come closer.

"You do not mean what you have just said, do you?" she asked slowly, with surprise written all over her face.

Adisa took the weight off his feet beside her and narrated how Johnny had seen Mira sneak out of the palace one night of the Ogoje festival.

"But can the words of a perpetual drunkard be taken seriously?" she asked after a while.

"Johnny was not drunk while he was saying it," he answered.

His wife stood up, thanked him for his undying love, and gave her word to stay away from the king's palace. Adisa smiled and hugged her before she departed.

4

The Expensive Joke

Soku remembered he had to go to the river to check *on* his fish traps at a time when the sun had hidden its glittery face in shame. It was a bad day for him, since none of the traps had caught any fish. He was in a bad mood. As he was returning from the river, he decided to spend some time at the *draft game centre*, so as to while away time before going home. He met Adisa and a friend playing while others were seated round them. These men cheered them on. He joined the observers, and they watched as the two parties played.

After some time Johnny arrived and refused to sit with others but did his observation while standing. Adisa defeated his friend twice, to the admiration of the observers. His friend was mocked and advised to quit the game. He stood up and boasted that he who fights and runs away lives to fight another day.

As soon as Soku settled down to play with Adisa, Johnny started laughing loudly until everyone shifted their attention towards him.

Adisa looked suggestively at him and asked, "What is wrong with you?"

"Do you want to play with this eunuch who shares his wife with another man?" he replied.

"Let me just try him; maybe he will be a different man at game," Adisa advised jokingly, as it is a tradition at draft centers to crack expensive joke.

Everyone laughed at the crude joke, except Soku, whose face had hardened.

"What kind of joke was that?" Soku asked furiously. "I love my wife so much that I cannot compromise her for anything in the world," he added.

Everyone laughed again, and some of them fell down while doing so. Johnny sat on the ground laughing foolishly.

Adisa tapped him on the shoulder and said, "Come on, man! Let's start, or what are you thinking? It may be possible you are a better man at game."

"Leave him alone and stop the sermon. This is not the right time and place for him to know the truth," Johnny said, facing Adisa.

Soku stood up slowly and walked away quietly in shame. They all laughed as he walked away. His ordeal remained the gist of the day at the draft game center. They gossiped and laughed, like men who were controlled by strong alcohol, as they played their game.

Soku rushed home angrily to confront his wife on the truth of the matter.

"She must leave my home today, if I find out the allegation is true," he thought as he entered his compound, shouting her name emphatically.

But to his greatest amazement, she was not at home. He was restless. He paced up and down the room like a wounded lion. At last, he took a stool, positioned it at the entrance, and sat on it. His whole body shook violently. He became angrier as he waited.

"I will wait for her until she meets me here," he thought.

While Soku waited, he dozed off and landed heavily on the ground. He quickly jumped up and found out it was midnight.

"Where could this woman be? What do I do? I had better go look for her. No, I should—." Just as he was contemplating on what to do, his wife sneaked in through the bamboo gate.

Soku accosted her and confronted her with what he had heard.

"Welcome, prostitute, where are you coming from by this time of the day?" he asked angrily.

"Why are you calling me a prostitute? After all, I am coming from the market," she answered casually.

"Market indeed! You are coming from the palace. Isn't it? You will leave this house today and join that shameless concubine of yours," he shouted.

They bartered abuses and shouted at each other. Neighbors started gathering round them.

"I have never been this humiliated in my life. You are raising false accusations against me," she said amidst torrents of tears.

"Do you know the meaning of false accusation?" her husband asked her, angrily nodding his head and shaking violently like an epileptic patient.

His neighbors pacified and cautioned him against beating his wife, no matter the circumstances. His wife threatened to report him to the king again, if he should lay his filthy hands on her again.

"This is what I have heard from several people. My ears are full, and my eardrums are about to explode. A lot of people have sung it into my ears since yesterday. So tell me, what is false about it?" He paused, looked intensely at her then continued with what he was saying. "You are a whore! Stupid human being! Go ahead and report me to that impotent lover of yours."

The neighbors that had gathered whispered among themselves while others stood some yards away to gossip.

Soku had a restless night, while his wife slept heavily. She woke up before daybreak and begged her husband. Soku loved his wife, so he had compassion and forgave her. He, however, warned her to desist from such a disgraceful act.

5

The Secret Plot

The next day, Mira sneaked into the king's palace again. She looked pale and dejected. His royal majesty asked what the problem was.

"It is Soku that …," she stammered.

"No! No! I do not want to hear anything about that useless fisherman. Must we discuss your irresponsible husband anytime we meet?" he asked.

"Hear me out, my lord, it is a different story this time, and it really has to do with you," Mira replied.

"How do you mean?" he asked uneasily.

"He is on the verge of letting the cat out of the bag. You need to see how he disgraced me yester-night before the whole community. He alleged I was having an affair with you," she said, with tears rolling down her cheeks.

"So, your husband wants to strip off my royal garment in the open," said the king. He stood up, sat down, and stood up again. She admonished him to be patient.

"I cannot take it easy. He is stepping on a python's tail. I have to get his coconut head chopped off from his body by tomorrow evening," he said angrily.

She knelt down and said, "No! My lord, if a child claims to be too wise, offer him an ant to slaughter with a mighty sword."

"What do you want me to do to him?" he asked as he waved his hand for her to rise up.

"My Lord, we have to be careful if we want to do anything." She whispered into the king's ear after a long silence, and he smiled.

"So, you women reason too?" His Royal Majesty said as he leaned his back against a weed-pillow and stared lustfully at her.

They entered an inner room and shut the door behind them. Several minutes later, she came out sweating profusely and adjusting her rumpled wrapper and tiptoed out as usual.

After about three market days, the king asked the town crier to announce to the entire community about a forthcoming fishing competition. Soku was indifferent to the competition, but his unrepentant, adulterous wife would not let him be. She reminded him of how poor they were and begged him to contest perchance they won; it could change their lives for the better. After several persuasions, he made up his mind, but in truth he never wanted anything to do with the unfaithful king. His love for his wife prompted him to always want to please her.

The great day came, and the fishermen went fishing from morning till sunset. It was a tedious event for the fishermen, but they were in a happy mode because it was a festive affair. They assembled

before the king in the evening with what they had caught. Soku's fish was not the biggest, and he knew he had lost in the competition.

King Zamadora examined all the fish carefully laid on the ground but announced Soku as the winner. Soku jumped up in excitement. All the people present cheered and congratulated him, though some were green with envy. King Zamadora decreed that the winner was to have the king's royal gold ring for six months, during which he would be entitled to share anything given to him equally—except his wives.

Soku and his wife were happy for this victory, and they both rejoiced.

Johnny wobbled toward them as they danced and said, "For dining with the devil, you must learn how to use a very long spoon."

They looked at him with scorn and continued dancing.

"Now I know you you are an enemy of progress," Mira shouted at Johnny and shook her buttocks in a funny routine to spite him.

Johnny shook his head and walked away. Meanwhile, King Zamadora was busy observing the rhythm of the vibration of Mira's buttocks. It was celebration galore at the palace until darkness enveloped the community.

… … … … … … … … … … … … … … …

For five and a half months, Soku lived as a king. The king's entitlements from the farmers, hunters, and artisans were divided into two equal parts, as well as taxes from taxpayer's money. He became wealthy. In the face of his wealth, he only went fishing every now and then. He was generous to all his neighbors.

A week to the day the golden ring was to be returned, Mira conspired with her lover to steal the ring and throw it into the river. They were happy with the ploy.

"Yes! Yes! It's high time he gets punished for his contempt to my person and the throne," King Zamadora said and hugged Mira for her ingenious ideas.

The moment the cock crowed, Soku jumped up, took his gourd and nets, and headed for the river. Mira waited for some time then stealthily took the gold ring from where her husband kept it and tied it to the tip of her wrapper. Without hesitation, she proceeded to the river at a time when her husband would be gone. She stood at the riverbank contemplating what to do with the royal ring. She gave it a second thought that it would be imprudent on her part to throw it in at the riverside. So she walked a few yards into the river and threw it into the middle of the river with all her might. She hurried home to avoid being queried by her husband.

Later that evening, she prepared a delicious meal, and her husband devoured it. He thanked her

for her unrelenting love as she flashed a mischievous smile at him.

"Your days are numbered," she thought as she smiled wickedly.

6

The Confrontation

The next day, Soku's wife tiptoed into the palace. She told the king that she had thrown the ring into the river. They were happy over their nefarious actions. They laughed and retired to their normal routine behind closed doors.

Three days to the end of the six months, Soku searched for the ring everywhere but could not find it. His wife joined in the search but all to no avail. He was confused and afraid.

"I am finished!" he stammered to his wife.

"Calm down, my husband, I know we will find it," she consoled her visibly tremulous husband. "I suggest we wait till morning and continue with the search. Everywhere is dark, and we cannot see properly."

They retired to their bamboo-made bed. His wife slept like a log of wood. Soku sat up till dawn, sleepless and tortured by the thought of what would happen to him if he did not find the gold ring. He was afraid of the wicked king. He prayed for the will of the Almighty Creator to be done.

At the first cock crow, he jumped out of bed, looking dejected as he continued the search without

his wife waking up. After a while, his wife woke up and joined him in the search. They frantically rummaged through the house, checking every nook and cranny. He sweated profusely, as cold as the morning breeze was.

"Oh! My God, what do I do to escape the wrath of His Royal Majesty?" he yelled then sat on the ground and started crying like a baby.

His wife stooped beside him, placed her left hand on his shoulder, and consoled him. She ultimately suggested he should go and inform the king.

"Probably he may have mercy on you and forget about the royal gold ring," she suggested, and her husband gave in.

Soku did as he was counseled. He came back with bad news; the king had given him an extra five days to provide the gold ring or his property would be confiscated and he would be cast out into the evil forest. Soku was depressed while his wife pretended to be sad, but deep down she was quite excited.

Momentarily, the king asked the town crier to summon all and sundry to the palace at a time when the smiling face of the sun had diminished. Soku's heart beat heavily as he walked toward the palace. He was scared to the bone marrow when he saw the huge crowd.

The king told the people, on their arrival, of what had happened. It was no longer news because the rumor about the missing ring had circulated in the whole community.

After a while, the king took a deep breath and swore, by his ancestors and the throne, before his subjects that if Soku failed to return the royal gold ring in seven days, he would be dealt with and thrown out of the community.

"Yes, I said it; a beautiful parrot that knows its feathers are in high demand should not build its nest close to the ground," Johnny said, swaying to and fro like a plant being controlled by the wind, as he moved away from the palace.

"I tried to caution him, but he would not listen to the voice of reasoning because of greed," he said to himself as he walked shakily past Adisa's buddy, who was just returning from his farmland.

He seemed to be surprised but managed to ask, "Who are you talking to?"

Johnny ignored him and walked away.

Since that day, Soku has been filled with unhappiness. He lost appetite for food and began to emaciate speedily. He was less worried about living in abject poverty than about being banished. Meanwhile, his two-faced wife was full of joy. She daydreamed of how life with the king in the palace would be after her wretched husband was banished.

Each visit she made to the palace was to make mockery of her husband.

"Your subject barely eats these days. He is growing thinner and thinner," she said to her secret lover on her frequent visits.

"Is he ill?" King Zamadora asked mockingly, laughing mischievously.

Mira laughed out loud too and said, "Ill indeed."

"He is sick over the missing ring, which he will never find," her lord said.

"Now tell me how he will survive this sickness of his," Mira said teasingly. They laughed again and fell over each other.

"Oh! My Lord, it is time I left, for that walking corpse will soon wake up. After next tomorrow, we shall have all the time in the world. A patient dog eats the fattest bone," she said as she took her leave.

King Zamadora watched as she wriggled her well-shaped buttocks up and down through the back door.

A day before the final day that Soku was to face the king's verdict, he went to the river. While at the river, he sat at the shore thinking of what next to do to avert the king's wrath. The past few days had been the worst he ever lived through. He felt he was caught in a trap and was waiting for the hunter to come along and finish him off.

When it was getting dark, he stood to go back home when he saw Johnny staggering to and fro toward him.

"What has this worthless drunkard come here to do? What does he want?" he murmured and stared deeply at him as if he was staring at a ghost.

"Is it a crime to see a friend and salute him? I have come to greet you," Johnny said as if he was

responding to his murmur. "My worried friend, give me fish. I have not eaten fish for a long time. A man who sits by the watercourse where fishermen make their catch will not eat plain food," Johnny requested, pretending to be unaware of what was happening to him.

Soku stared suggestively at him and replied, "I have not come here to fish today."

"Why then do you have your net in the river?" he queried authoritatively, drawing Soku's attention to the net in the river.

He was amazed. He had left the net in his canoe at the shore three days ago. He thought the net must have gotten into the river. He then remembered that there was a heavy downpour that night, and so he concluded the wind must have blown it into the river.

He reluctantly entered the canoe and paddled it to where the net was, while Johnny watched with keen interest. He paddled back with the net, which had just one fish in it, but it was a big one. Gladly, he gave the fish to Johnny and returned to his sitting position. Johnny thanked him and walked unsteadily home.

Soku stared at him as he departed. He waited till the moon peered all the way through the sky and smiled at him on the riverbank. He gazed at the sapphire glittering on the water for a moment. His mind drifted to the beauty of nature, but the burden in his heart would not let him feel the soothing nature of it. After a moment, he went home with a broken spirit.

7

The Judgment Day

The day came when all the dwellers had assembled at the palace. The king was not seated yet, but Soku prostrated before the throne waiting for his verdicts. After a long wait King Zamadora came out, and all paid obeisance. It seemed like the longest wait of Soku's life. He panicked at the appearance of His Royal Majesty and was frozen with fear at the sight of the dreaded ruler, making the hairs on the nape of his neck rise.

King Zamadora addressed the community dwellers. "The gods of our land know I have passed the acid test because you have not been able to provide my gold ring at the agreed time. At least I have given you five additional days. Now I shall pronounce my judgment."

Mira ran in, wailing like a lunatic being tormented by unseen forces. The women and the men pitied her, while some of them, who knew about her clandestine affair with the randy king, mocked her.

King Zamadora ignored her and continued, "As I had earlier promised that if Soku can provide the gold ring before five days, he shall be the king. If he

fails, he shall be banished into the evil forest, and so shall I do now."

The inhabitants looked at each other, as Soku sobbed like a baby craving for breast milk. King Zamadora ordered that Soku be stripped naked before being escorted to the evil forest, and his wife should stay in the palace, as tradition stipulates that all widows belong to the king. Mira wailed that she should be banished with her husband. She begged the king amidst torrents of tears to have mercy on her husband, as the guards seized Soku. Johnny staggered in with a bottle of local gin underneath his left armpit.

He stared at everyone and said, "The hen that pecks on a rock must trust the strength of its beak."

Everyone ignored him except Adisa, who was in the crowd.

"The sky is large enough for every bird to fly without colliding with each other. Can't you see we are not in good moods and you are before our able king?" Adisa asked sarcastically.

Johnny ignored him and danced happily to the astonishment of each and every one. He had consistently been a good dancer years back. Everyone laughed except Soku, Mira, Adisa, and Pa Koiki.

Adisa's wife gazed scornfully at him and retorted, "He is a complex fool and has no knowledge of himself. *What—*"

He interrupted her and said, "Is it your late father, who fell down from the palm tree, you are

talking to? May you and your husband be knocked down by a palm-wine taper's bicycle."

It was laughing galore at the palace and even Soku, the man on death row, was not left out. But he was restrained by his predicament.

Momentarily, Pa Koiki ordered everyone to remain silent. He also asked them if they had no respect for His Royal Highness.

Immediately, the people returned to the matter at hand. King Zamadora watched with keen interest from his throne.

"The palm-wine taper is a subject to a palm-wine seller, while he remains a king to the drunkard. This is not the right place for me to be at this moment. My palace is at Mama Akpan's place, but before I leave, no one can banish Soku from this noble township," Johnny said finally, with a tone of seriousness.

They were startled at his audacity in challenging the king. King Zamadora chuckled. He was beginning to lose his temper. He rose from his throne with the swiftness of an angry lion on its prey and asked him what he had just said. He said it again without a hitch. Many onlookers feared that Johnny had come to his end by challenging the king's words openly. King Zamadora was taken aback but managed to ask him what his reason was. He responded by saying that he had found the missing ring. Soku jumped up then prostrated again when he realized he was before the king, chiefs, and elders.

"Could it be true?" he thought as his heart pounded faster than ever.

Everyone was stunned. Adisa and his spouse glanced at each other and smiled mockingly.

"The words of a drunkard cannot be taken seriously," Adisa's wife whispered again.

"Yes, my dear, you are right." Her husband concurred by nodding his head.

"I will teach you a bitter lesson that the beards of elders is not for child's play. If you have come here to deceive me and my subjects, you had better have a rethink," King Zamadora threatened.

"Yes! Yes!" they agreed.

"It cannot be true. He must be joking," Mira thought.

"So what have you for us, shameless drunkard?" the king asked mockingly.

Without mincing words, Johnny dipped his feeble hand into his left pocket and brought out the ring to the surprise of everyone present. Mira was enveloped with fear as beads of sweat rolled down her forehead. She was restless. The chiefs and elders were thunderstruck. There was absolute calmness.

After a while, King Zamadora managed to challenge Johnny on the legitimacy of the gold ring. The chiefs and the elders took a cautious look at the gold ring and confirmed it after several consultations among themselves. Pa Akpamurere, the well-known goldsmith, was also asked to confirm the genuineness of the gold ring.

"This was the royal gold ring my forefathers manufactured for King Zamadora's forefathers before he was born," he said, and returned it to the most senior chief then took his seat among the crowd.

Silence enveloped the palace again. Soku lay calmly before the king, praying in his heart that if this was a dream, he should not be woken up from it. His Highness gazed fiercely at Mira. She could not bear the look; rather she looked away in frustration.

"But I thought you said he will never find it," His Majesty uttered out of desperation as he made to attack Mira, who knelt down beside her spouse.

The elders and chiefs promptly stopped him.

"Ha! So you knew about it?" the people exclaimed with mouths opened.

They were ashamed of the sacrilege committed by the royal father of the land on the sacred throne. Though they were aware of his sinful behavior, none had been made public. Soku was shocked at his wife's involvement and shook his head in disappointment. She could not dare to look at him but instead looked away in shame. Meanwhile, Johnny sat down quietly on the ground, vindicated, and watched the sudden turn of events. King Zamadora and Mira felt defeated.

8

The Boomerang

The people were bitter. There were mutterings concerning the king's immoral and tyrannical leadership. Immediately, Ladi's wife mobilized the women while his children incited the youths. The men were not left out. They chanted war songs. King Zamadora was too confused to utter a word. He was dazed at the sudden revelation.

The elders and the chiefs tried to calm the people. The eldest chief rose and ordered Soku to sit near him. Soku pleaded with the chiefs and the elders to ask Johnny to explain how he came about the missing gold ring. Johnny explained, to the astonishment of everyone, how he had opened the belly of the fish given to him by Soku the night before and found the ring in it.

"Yes! It is good to be generous," Adisa said.

"How do you mean, my dear?"

"I mean, one good turn deserves another," he answered.

"You are right," one of the onlookers responded.

Pa Koiki turned to King Zamadora and said, "We are highly disappointed in you. You are supposed to be the custodian of our tradition."

"And you," he said facing Mira, "are an eyesore to your family, a disgrace to humanity, a shame to womanhood, and a disappointment to this great community. You conspired with the king to harm your own husband because of your frivolous act." Some of the women hissed and spat away.

His disgraceful majesty looked away in shame while Mira could not hold herself any longer. She burst into tears and confessed her amorous affairs with the king and how the king had asked her to throw the ring into the middle of the river so that her husband could be banished.

"I knew it was a dreadful thing to do," she went on, "but I sincerely ask for your forgiveness."

"Banish her! Banish her!" the people yelled.

"She is perhaps one of the most undisciplined, immoral, and unpleasant women I have ever met," Pa Koiki whispered.

"If you probe into her past, you will find this out for yourselves. She was utterly rotten," Johnny the drunkard added.

"Why do you have to betray your husband?" one of the elders asked her irritably.

"He made me do it, so that he can have me to himself," she said and buried her face in her palms.

"Ha! Adulterous woman," they screamed again.

"You should not trust a man or a woman who says that the hippopotamus is not an ugly animal. Justice to one is justice to all," Pa Koiki said.

After listening carefully, the people protested the more. They asked King Zamadora to give up the throne and be banished from the community with his concubine, so they would continue their love affair in the evil forest.

"Yes! Yes!" they all concurred.

"A farmer will regard a yam tendril that has the support of leaves. If by any reason our king betrays the confidence of our noble people, then the appropriate step must be taken by the council of elders and chiefs," one of the elders said. He assured everyone that a decision would be reached as soon as possible.

The councils of chiefs and elders excused themselves. His Royal Highness was short of words. He blinked several times like a thief caught in a sugar cane plantation.

"How terribly wrong everything has gone," Mira thought as she knelt down and covered her face with her shaky hands.

He gazed at her gravely and looked away as tears began to trickle through her fingers. Beads of perspiration stood out on her forehead. She was heavy-hearted. For the first time in her whole life, she was faced with the indisputable reality that she could not eat her cake and have it. But once she harbored this thought, she was mortally afraid of it. She tried to thrust it away from her and face the consequences. It was too late to cry when the head was already cut off. It is much too late to regret anything. She gave her

husband a quick glance, bit hard at her lower lip, and then made a gesture of hopelessness.

Soku glanced back without a word, but after a moment his mind ruminated through the issue as he sat down quietly, with jubilation in his heart.

He shook his head and said, "Why was it all going to end this way? The greatest native doctor prophesied that she was the best woman for me. Even my parents and relatives were adamant that I should marry her or no one else."

He was terrified of the ultimate humiliation his wife had brought on him and his family. But he knew that it was impossible for him to continue loving her with the blind passion of earlier days. He was frozen with an unknown fear. His spirit, already very low, dropped to zero. He faced the fact that there could be no revival of that first love for her, never again could he feel that first blind ecstasy that had been his when he married her. Because then he had believed in her, respected her, adored her, and now there was nothing left to respect.

"The most disloyal woman in the world can be forgiven for any act of disloyalty but certainly not for the sacrilegious deed committed by her," he said coldly and firmly to her.

She knelt down silently, breathing quickly, her eyes shut for a moment. She listened with swimming eyes. And through the curtain of tears, she looked at his face and read what lay in those passionate eyes of her husband.

She beseeched her husband, but he would not listen.

"I'd like you to remember that there is no woman in the world whom I would have liked to have had for my wife as much as you, but you betrayed my love," her spouse responded amidst her moans and then turned away coldly.

Soku was happy he had regained his life. The people rained curses on Mira while others muttered foul words at the king.

Johnny stood up and shouted that, "Justice must be done. Justice delayed is justice denied. We want justice." At that, the crowd shouted they wanted justice to be done. King Zamadora was scared when he saw the anger in the people's eyes. He made an attempt to escape, but the palace guards promptly stopped him. Meanwhile, all of the king's wives and his only daughter had escaped through the back door. They ran to the neighboring community to seek asylum.

After a brief consultation with each other, the chiefs and the elders entered. Pa Koiki, the head of the council, thanked the good people of Imoku community and delivered the verdict.

"The council has decided that Zamadora ceases to be our king," he said with all his might as he took a deep breath.

There was a loud ovation and jubilation by the people. Soku and others flashed victorious smiles. King Zamadora felt like the whole of heaven had collapsed on him. He could not imagine himself

falling from grace to grass. His eyes were filled with tears pleading to be let out.

"Oh! What a disgraceful way to lose my birthright and generational inheritance," he thought.

Pa Koiki continued, "We have also decided not to pass judgment on them."

There was sudden disappointment on the faces of everyone, especially Johnny and Soku. They stopped jubilating as their countenances hardened, while the culprits' faces brightened.

"But we shall use the verdict against them." He paused, ordered the guards to arrest them and strip them nude, and continued. "I do hereby decree the verdict that they should be banished to the evil forest."

They both looked at each other in fear mixed with shame. There was excitement and relief as the verdict was delivered. Soku and his savior hugged each other. The people sang and danced.

"At last! The gods of our land finally answered our pleas after all these years," Ladi's widow said.

"But what took the gods of the land so long to intervene in our community?" one of the women asked with a look of mystery on her face.

"You are right, my daughter, the gods are not sleeping. They gave him time to repent, but he failed to listen. The gods are wise, but they are not as wise as the Almighty Creator that created him. He gave him a pure heart to love and serve his people, but he corrupted it with the mundane things of this world," Pa Koiki uttered.

"Baba, you are right; may you live long for your wonderful wisdom," she prayed.

Everyone was happy except Zamadora and Mira.

"And our final judgment is that Soku be made our king in two market days," Pa Koiki said with a tone of finality.

Soku was dazzled, and tears of joy rolled down his cheeks. After weeping for a while, he refused the kingship offer, but the chiefs, elders and the villagers persuaded him. He later had a rethink.

"You made me lose my matrimonial home," the miserable concubine alleged amidst tears.

"Shut up! You are a shameless harlot. You made me lose my family and the throne. You seduced me with your sexy bottom," he uttered amidst tears too.

"It is a lie. You forced me to have an affair with you," she uttered angrily.

The guards ordered them to be silent as they were being escorted into the evil forest.

"There they shall be devoured by wild beasts," Adisa's wife thought as her friend was being led away. Though she felt for her wayward friend, there was nothing she could do to help.

Soku could not stand his adulterous wife being led away. He pleaded with the good people of Imoku and the council of elders and chiefs to have mercy on them. They vehemently refused. It took the elders and chiefs a while to put the people in order. After

much consultation between the chiefs and elders, they finally agreed to exile them.

Soku invited all to his tattered home that smelled of fish to feast with him. They danced to his home and celebrated his victory over death and his forthcoming coronation. Adisa and his wife were also present.

Johnny became a celebrated hero. His friendship with the king-elect became so strong that they were always seen together. His life changed from being a drunk to a responsible person, while his new friend turned from being a fisherman to the most respected man in the community and beyond.

Two market days later, Soku was crowned the paramount ruler of Imoku Community. It was celebration galore in the community and beyond. The people of the community felt liberated from the tyranny of the exiled king. Joy was let loose, and peace smiled at everyone. There was plenty to eat and drink. The less privileged took the leftovers home.

A few days later, Soku made Johnny his special adviser.

King Soku married the erstwhile king's daughter shortly before the coronation. He ruled the people with love, and peace reigned all over the kingdom.

Printed in the United States
By Bookmasters